DISCARDED

EARTH'S CHANGING LANDSCAPE

Weather & Climate

John Corn

A+

First published in 2004 by Franklin Watts
Franklin Watts, 96 Leonard Street, London EC2A 4XD

Franklin Watts Australia
45-51 Huntley Street, Alexandria, NSW 2015
This edition published under license from Franklin Watts. All rights reserved.

Copyright © 2004 Franklin Watts

Series Editor: Sarah Peutrill; Series Designer: Simon Borrough; Art Director: Jonathan Hair; Picture Researchers: Juliet Duff and Diana Morris; Series Consultant: Steve Watts, FRGS, Principal Lecturer in Geography Education at the University of Sunderland

Published in the United States by Smart Apple Media
1980 Lookout Drive, North Mankato, Minnesota 56003

U.S. publication copyright © 2005 Smart Apple Media
International copyright reserved in all countries. No part of this book may be reproduced in any form without written permission from the publisher.

Library of Congress Control Number: 2004102618

ISBN 1-58340-478-3

9 8 7 6 5 4 3 2 1

Picture credits:
Andrew Brown/Ecoscene: 9, 11, 32, 36, 37, 38. Christiana Carvalho/FLPA: 18, 25. John Corbett/Ecoscene: 22. Eric Crichton/Corbis: 7b. James Davis Worldwide: 8. Nigel Dickinson/Still Pictures: 16b. Digital Vision: 14, 15t, 19, 30-31, 38 inset, 39, 42. Mark Edwards/Still Pictures: 15b. David Hoadley/FLPA: front cover, 17. Keystone Praha/Rex: 13. John Kieffer/Still Pictures: 28. Frans Lanting/Minden/FLPA: 21. Brigitte Marcon/Still Pictures: 27. Sally Morgan/Ecoscene: 10. NASA: 16t, 43. Fritz Polking/Ecoscene: 24. Francois Savigny/Still Pictures: 7t. Erik Schaffer/Ecoscene: 40. Sipa/Rex: 12, 29. Paul Thompson/Eye Ubiquitous: 33. S. Tiwari/Ecoscene: 41.Brian A. Vikander/Corbis: 35. W Wisniewski/FLPA: 26. Gunter Ziesler/Still Pictures: 34.

CONTENTS

What is weather?	6
Weathering	8
Erosion	10
Floods	12
Drought	14
Hurricanes and tornadoes	16
El Niño	18
What is climate?	20
Past and present climates	22
Polar regions	24
Taiga (northern forests)	26
Mountains	28
Temperate regions	30
Mediterranean climate	32
Tropical grasslands (savanna)	34
Deserts	36
Rainforests	38
Monsoon lands	40
The future	42
Glossary	44
Further information	45
Index	46

WHAT IS WEATHER?

Weather refers to what is happening in the **atmosphere** at the moment. It is concerned with temperature, rainfall, wind speed, wind direction, sunshine, and clouds. The weather can alter the **landscape** dramatically in a few hours through extreme phenomenon such as hurricanes, but it can also change it very slowly over time through weathering and erosion.

Ever changing Weather changes constantly. In a few minutes, temperatures may rise or fall, the wind may increase or decrease in speed and change direction. Clouds may build up to obscure the sun or clear away to reveal bright sunshine.

The atmosphere Weather is caused by the air that surrounds the planet, called the atmosphere, cooling down and warming up. The atmosphere is made of five layers. Weather happens only in the layer that is nearest to Earth.

The sun The sun is an important influence on the weather. The sun's rays warm Earth's surface, and this then heats the air above it. Earth moves slowly around the sun once every year. Different places become closer to the sun through the year, which causes the different weather patterns called seasons. In different climates (*see pages 24–41*), the weather brought about by the seasons has a major effect on Earth's landscape.

Air pressure Air pressure—which is caused by gravity—also affects what the weather will be like. Low air pressure usually indicates cloudy, rainy weather. High air pressure usually indicates sunny, clear weather.

This early morning mist has been caused by low pressure. The sun's rays are less powerful because they have to shine through the mist to warm Earth's surface.

Follow it through: the Sirocco — Hot, dry air moves north from the Sahara — It meets cooler, **humid** air over the Mediterranean

Clouds

Clouds reduce the amount of energy reaching Earth from the sun during the day. They stop much of the warm air from escaping at night, acting like a "cloud blanket." Places that have a lot of clouds experience only small changes in their daytime and nighttime temperatures compared with places, such as deserts, where cloud cover is much less.

Wind

Wind is caused by air in Earth's atmosphere moving from one place to another. The air moves from areas of high pressure to low pressure. The pressure differences are caused by the sun heating up the air. Warm air is lighter, so it rises, creating low pressure. Cool air is heavier, so it sinks and creates high pressure.

Wind can have both long-term and short-term effects on the landscape. Over a long time, trees on windy hillsides grow more leaves on their sheltered sides, away from the wind. Winds can also be massively powerful and cause sudden destruction to a landscape.

With little cloud cover, this desert receives hot temperatures during the day and cold temperatures at night.

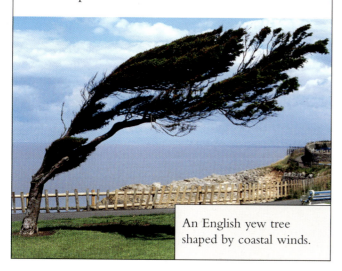
An English yew tree shaped by coastal winds.

Case study: the Sirocco

There are different types of wind depending on location; for example, coastal winds and mountain-valley winds. There are also desert winds, such as the Sirocco.

The Sirocco is a southerly wind that draws in hot air from a large area of the northern Sahara Desert, normally in the spring and early summer. The air passes over the Mediterranean Sea, which is about 18 °F (10 °C) cooler but far more humid. When these two air masses meet, heavy rain and thunderstorms develop, and winds can reach more than 30 miles (50 km) per hour.

The resulting heavy storms may reach the European shores of the Mediterranean Sea, causing damage to crops. Local people often complain about headaches, depression, and sleeping problems. The air contains large quantities of sand and dust, much of which comes down with the rain. This dust has been found as far north as the Netherlands.

| Storms and heavy rain develop | Strong winds occur | There is damage to crops |

WEATHERING

Many things, when they are left outside, begin to break down: metal rusts, wood cracks, and even the stones on ancient buildings or gravestones show signs of decay. This is because they have been exposed to the weather.

What is weathering?

Weathering describes the processes through which rock and other materials are broken down by the weather. The process begins as soon as new material is exposed to the atmosphere. It will take several hundred years for lettering on gravestones to become unreadable. And over thousands or millions of years, weathering can have a dramatic effect on the landscape.

Physical weathering

"Frost wedging" occurs when water expands as it freezes, enlarging cracks in rocks and causing them to split over time. When this happens, chunks of rock break away, and on steep valley sides, they may accumulate to form "scree."

Rocks heated by the sun expand during the day, but at night, they cool and contract. This causes cracks to appear in their surface. Eventually, layers of rock will "peel off" and fall to the ground. These are called "exfoliation domes." This is a common process in desert areas that experience extreme temperatures during the day.

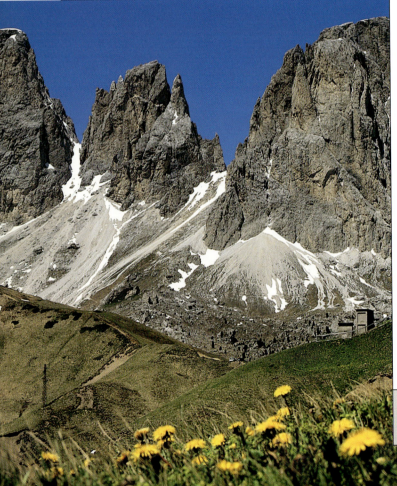

Scree has formed on the sides of this mountain in Italy.

Follow it through: rock changes → Rocks heated by the sun expand during the day → Rocks cool and contract at night

Take it further
Find out about a limestone landscape using the Internet.

◆ Download some of the information and photographs you find and make a leaflet advertising the area and its scenery.
◆ Display these with maps and other tourist information that you can find.

Chemical weathering
Carbon dioxide, which is a gas contained in the air, dissolves in rainwater and makes it slightly acidic. This **acid rain** will react with minerals in rocks over time and either dissolve them or turn them into other minerals.

The features that are produced as a result of chemical weathering can be dramatic. In the Yorkshire Dales in the UK, there are large areas of "limestone pavement"—exposed limestone that is covered with deep gulleys created by rainwater. There are also "swallow holes"—gaps in the limestone through which rivers may disappear into cave systems. There, water slowly trickling through the limestone evaporates to leave deposits of calcium in the form of **stalagmites** and **stalactites**. Over time, the walls of an underground cave will enlarge so much that its roof will collapse to form a steep-sided **gorge**.

Over thousands of years, acidic rainwater has dissolved weak areas of the limestone to create deep cracks at Malham Cove, Yorkshire, UK.

Rocks become unstable → Rocks crack and peel → They form smaller rock fragments, sand, and dust

EROSION

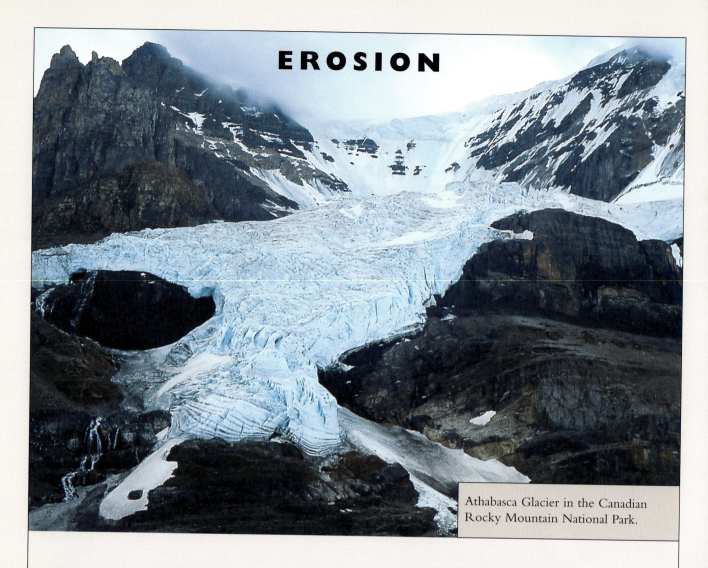

Athabasca Glacier in the Canadian Rocky Mountain National Park.

Erosion occurs when particles of rock and soil are loosened by weathering, or by physical means, and begin to move. This is usually due to the action of **glaciers**, wind, or water. It is possible to find evidence of erosion in most landscapes, because it is responsible for the creation of hills, valleys, coasts, and many other features.

Glaciation Glaciers and ice sheets cover about 10 percent of Earth's surface. Ice sheets are areas of seawater that are frozen to a great depth. They are mostly found in the polar regions. Smaller glaciers of compact ice and snow occur in high **mountain** ranges.

During the **ice age** (*see page 22*), ice sheets and mountain glaciers expanded to cover much of northern Europe and America and carved the landscape into the form we see today.

Follow it through: glaciers → Snow and ice accumulate in a hollow on a mountainside → Snow compacts into hard ice

Glacier formation

Glaciers are formed in armchair-like hollows known as "corries," way up in the mountains. Over hundreds of years, snow builds up in the hollows, and because of the cold and weight of snow, it gradually turns to ice. These huge blocks of ice are then drawn by gravity down the mountain valley. They erode the sides and make the valley into a U-shape.

Rock fragments of all sizes are dragged along, and they scour the land and remove huge quantities of soil, heaping it along the sides and front of the glacier as "moraine." In the summer, glaciers melt a little, creating meltwater streams that flow down the mountainsides into the valleys below.

Wind Wind is an important agent of erosion. In places that are dry with loose soil, such as deserts, the wind picks up particles of dust and sand and uses them to sand-blast boulders into smooth, rounded shapes. Rock faces are often undercut because the particles of sand are carried into the air only three to six feet (1–2 m).

Sand grains blown by the wind can form drifts or dunes in the shape of ridges and crescents, which slowly move in the direction of the wind.

An arch formed by wind erosion in Arches National Park, Utah.

Water Rivers also cause erosion, particularly after heavy rain. Rivers carry weathered material, such as soil and stones, so that over time, river valleys are made deeper and wider by erosion. As a river passes over rocks of different hardness, it erodes them at different speeds, which helps to produce a variety of landforms, including **rapids**, gorges, **waterfalls**, and **meanders**.

Hard ice eventually becomes so heavy that it begins to move ▶ The glacier erodes the valley sides, creating a U-shaped valley ▶ Rock and soil, eroded from the valley, form moraines in front of the glacier

FLOODS

Floods are an extreme weather event, and can occur for many reasons. Usually, they occur after a long spell of heavy rain when rivers cannot cope with the volume of water. Evidence based on rising sea temperatures and average land temperatures suggests that floods will become more common in the future.

Major impact

Floods can cause tremendous changes to the landscape, especially if they occur without warning. A few inches of water inside a house will ruin furnishings, plasterwork, and decorations, and damage the electricity supply. Twenty inches (50 cm) of fast-flowing water has the power to move cars, knock people down, and sweep them away. Within a few minutes, floods can destroy bridges and buildings, roll cars, and uproot trees.

Mudslides

Heavy rain falling in areas of high land or on steep ground can cause mudslides and landslides. When heavy rain soaks deep into the ground, it loosens the rocks and soil beneath. Under the force of gravity, the ground collapses and moves quickly down the slope, often taking trees and, sometimes, houses with it.

A mudslide in Italy, caused by heavy rain.

Coastal flooding

Floods can also occur when a storm sweeps across a coastline or when a **hurricane** reaches land. Flash floods—sudden, intense torrential rain—can also cause flooding.

One example of this, combined with coastal erosion, is of the Holbeck Hall Hotel in Scarborough, UK. There, trees that had been planted to hold the soil in place in front of the hotel had been removed so that guests could enjoy the view along the coast toward the town. As time passed, the land became more and more unstable until one morning in 1993, after heavy rain, guests woke to find that the hotel was slowly collapsing into the sea.

Case study: European floods, 2002

In August 2002, Central and Eastern Europe suffered widespread flooding after freak storms and prolonged heavy rainfall.

Prague

One of the first places to be swamped by the floodwater was Prague, in the Czech Republic. There, the river Vltava rose between four and six inches (10–15 cm) an hour to a total of 26 feet (8 m) above its usual height. It eventually stopped just two feet (60 cm) below the level of the sandbags hastily built to protect the old town near the center of Prague.

Austria, Germany, and Russia

Floodwaters also soaked parts of Austria, where thousands of people fought to protect Vienna from the advancing waters of the Danube. In Germany, a dam built in the southeast of the country burst, sending the waters of the river Mulde cascading toward the town of Bitterfeld. Its 16,000 inhabitants were quickly evacuated. Bridges became impassable as huge areas of the countryside were submerged under muddy brown water. Russia was one of the hardest hit countries. There, many tourists on the Black Sea coast were swept away by raging waters.

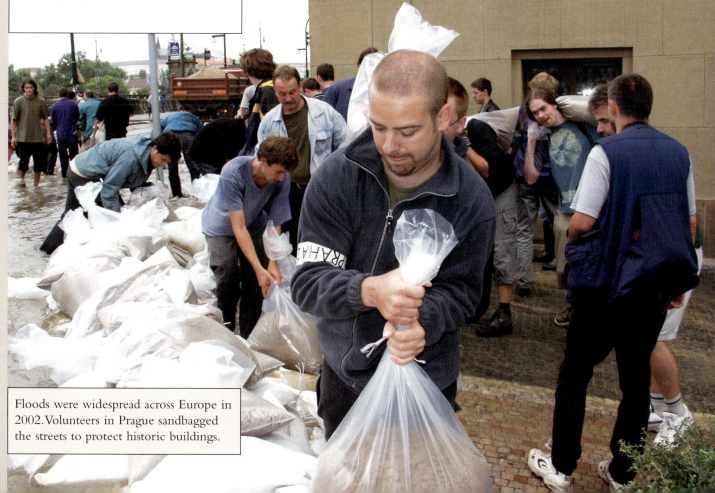

Floods were widespread across Europe in 2002. Volunteers in Prague sandbagged the streets to protect historic buildings.

DROUGHT

Drought can happen almost anywhere in the world from time to time. Drought is a temporary absence of rainfall. If it lasts long enough, farming, industry, and people may suffer from water shortages.

How bad? Droughts tend to be more severe in some areas than in others. Catastrophic droughts generally occur in areas closer to the **equator** and located near desert regions (*see map on page 23*). These droughts occur when dry desert air moves northward, making nearby areas drier than normal.

The effects In countries with only small amounts of rainfall and high evaporation, prolonged drought can cause real problems, especially if the countries are poor. In the mid-1980s, parts of Ethiopia, Sudan, Somalia, and Eritrea received no rain but had scorching temperatures for months. As a result, the landscape changed from one of lush green grasslands to a brown, dry, desert-like landscape with no pasture. Some of the land did not even recover when rain finally began to fall. Animals' hooves had churned up the soil, killing the grasses and plants so that the vegetation could not grow again. These areas turned into desert.

Without tree and plant roots to hold the soil together after a drought, soil erosion is a common problem.

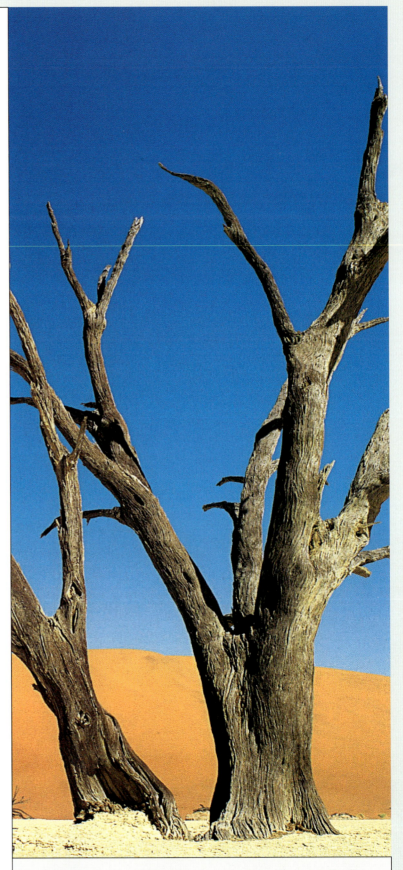

If a drought is prolonged, vegetation and trees will eventually die, and the area will turn into desert.

Surviving drought In some countries, people have to walk long distances to collect water during droughts, particularly if they have animals to look after.

Other countries, such as Egypt, have found new water sources for people to use and irrigate their land. Large **irrigation** systems, run from a network of canals close to the Aswan Dam on the Nile, allow fruit, vegetables, and crops to be grown in areas that were once desert.

In Saudi Arabia, desalinated water from the sea is used to irrigate the land. In Sinai, "trickle irrigation" from a system of plastic pipes has turned hundreds of acres of dry land into a huge market garden, producing oranges, apricots, and even roses. Good drainage in these areas is essential, otherwise the ground will become waterlogged. Standing water will evaporate and leave a buildup of natural salts in which new plants will not grow.

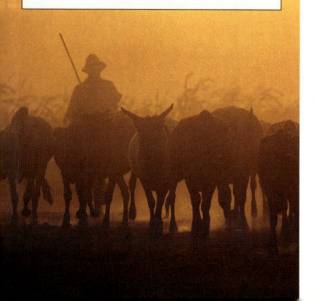

A Masai livestock farmer in Tanzania travels to find water in an area affected by drought.

A Sri Lankan tree house, built to protect a family from elephants.

Case study: Sri Lanka

Southern Sri Lanka suffered from a partial drought between 1996 and 2002. For 22 months, throughout 2001 and much of 2002, almost no rain fell. Most of the rivers, reservoirs, ponds, and wells dried up, and water carried through pipes was available for only a few hours each day. Fresh water had to be supplied to thousands of people in the worst affected areas.

Effect on the landscape
The tropical landscape changed from being lush and green to dry and gray. In some small villages, families had to sleep in tree houses because they were afraid of being attacked and trampled by elephants as they came into villages looking for food and water.

Drought ends
A return to "normal" weather brought the drought to an end in the final months of 2002. The following year saw plenty of rain and a record-breaking rice crop. Some areas even suffered from flooding.

HURRICANES AND TORNADOES

Hurricanes and **tornadoes** are violent weather phenomena that can have sudden and devastating effects on the landscape.

A hurricane as seen from space.

Hurricanes Hurricanes are violent, whirling storms, which can be up to 300 miles (500 km) wide. Winds circulate around them at speeds of more than 70 miles (120 km) per hour. They begin over warm oceans in areas of low pressure. The air swirls around the low pressure center and the winds get stronger. Near the central "eye," wind speeds of up to 190 miles (300 km) per hour can occur.

Hurricanes are called "typhoons" when they occur in the western Pacific Ocean, "cyclones" over the Indian Ocean, and "willy willies" in Australia. About six to eight tropical storms each year reach hurricane status.

A banana plantation in Honduras destroyed by Hurricane Mitch in 1998.

Follow it through: hurricane development → Tropical wind near West Africa → It moves west, gathers strength by the energy released from water vapor over the ocean, and becomes a tropical storm

Storm surge As a hurricane moves toward the coast, the wind and rain combine with the force of the sea to produce a huge tide called a "storm surge," which can often reach a good distance above normal sea level.

High winds and torrential rain—2.2 billion tons (2 billion t) of which may fall in a day—combined with the storm surge cause flooding and damage to coasts. Trees are uprooted, houses are wrecked, and communications are disrupted. Once over land, however, hurricanes cannot continue to draw their power from the warm ocean, and they eventually die out.

Tornadoes Tornadoes, or "twisters" as they are sometimes called, are the most violent weather systems known on Earth. These violent spinning funnels of air develop in turbulent storm clouds between quickly rising and falling air. They normally develop toward the end of a hot day. The winds of a tornado can reach speeds of more than 190 miles (300 km) per hour, but they may last for only a few minutes.

Building wreckers The most severe tornadoes occur in the midwestern U.S. in the late spring and early summer. There, about 700 are reported each year. They rip through the landscape, making a noise like an express train, destroying virtually everything in their path. Because of the differences in air pressure, buildings they pass through appear to explode, and cars, animals, and people are whisked into the air, often landing miles away.

Tornadoes are dramatic and terrifying sights.

Case study: Hurricane Floyd

Hurricane Floyd started out as a tropical wave, an area of curved cloud, near the Cape Verde Islands in the Atlantic Ocean close to West Africa on September 2, 1999. It surged through several U.S. states and Canada before finally dying out in the North Atlantic Ocean on September 19.

Destruction

Floyd's visit cost the lives of 74 people and caused more than $6 billion in damage. About 7,000 homes were destroyed, 17,000 were made uninhabitable, and 56,000 were damaged. Most crops in its path were ruined, roads were washed out, thousands of trees were uprooted, and landslides were set off.

Floods spread across North Carolina, inundating fields, roads, and houses. Many people spent several days on their rooftops waiting to be rescued.

| As more energy is released, winds increase to hurricane strength | Over land, winds cause severe damage | Winds begin to weaken over land where there is no more energy from evaporating water | Hurricane dies out |

EL NIÑO

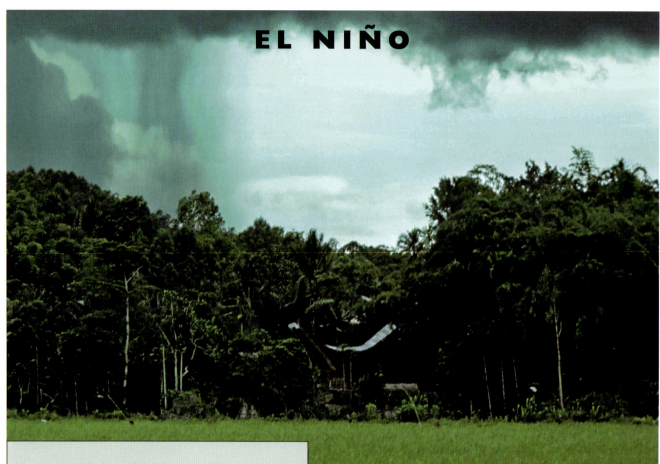

Some experts believe that heavy rainfall in Indonesia is caused by El Niño.

El Niño is a regularly occurring phenomenon which is believed to affect the weather across much of the planet. It has been linked with droughts in southern and eastern Africa and Asia, as well as unusual weather in parts of the U.S., causing floods and mudslides.

What is it? El Niño is a huge area of warm water, which usually lasts for about four years off the coast of South America. It then slowly crosses the Pacific, where it stays for another four years. Unusually cold ocean currents that occur when El Niño is not present are called "La Niña."

Scientists believe that El Niños and La Niñas have occurred for about the last 15,000 years, but the phenomenon was only discovered in the 1970s. The 18 °F (10 °C) temperature difference between El Niño and La Niña affects the temperature of the entire Pacific Ocean and weather systems across much of Earth.

Follow it through: El Niño and La Niña	West Pacific El Niño	Rise in sea temperatures
	East Pacific La Niña	Fall in sea temperatures

What happens? When warm water is near Indonesia, the air above is warmed and rises, clouds develop, and the area receives heavy rainfall. On the other side of the Pacific, the water is cool, the air above cannot hold much water, and dry conditions are created. But places such as Indonesia can suffer climatic extremes, with heavy rainfall being replaced by drought when the warm water moves away.

Affecting weather around the world In 2002, El Niño is thought to have caused a tornado that ripped through central Florida. Winds of up to 210 miles (340 km) per hour destroyed more than 200 buildings. At the same time, other tornadoes were touching down along the Atlantic and Gulf coasts of the state. Later, torrential rain fell for a month in northern California, where extensive flooding and mudslides caused $300 million worth of damage.

The effect of El Niño outside the U.S. was even more severe. Two hundred people were killed and 240,000 made homeless in storms in Peru. In Indonesia, a prolonged drought made forests dry, and fires, fanned by high winds, burned out of control. The fires and their thick smog were responsible for the deaths of 420 people, the destruction of crops, and later on, disease and famine were caused by the destruction of local water supplies.

Dry weather brought about by El Niño may be the cause of highly destructive forest fires.

El Niño research A major focus of research is to predict El Niño events so that governments are better prepared to tackle these kinds of catastrophes when they happen. Governments all over the world are developing emergency procedures and stockpiling resources, such as medicines and tents, to help them deal efficiently with a whole range of El Niño-related extreme weather events.

| Rise in air temperatures | Buildup of clouds | Heavy rain events | Flooding |
| Fall in air temperatures | Few clouds produced | Arid events | Drought |

WHAT IS CLIMATE?

Climate is the average weather pattern a place receives over at least 30 years. Unlike weather, which can have a sudden impact, a region's climate shapes and alters the landscape over time. It gives a place its character, such as dry, sandy deserts or lush, green rainforests. The climate a place has depends on its distance from the equator, distance from the sea, and height above sea level.

The equator Places closer to the equator heat up more quickly and have higher temperatures than places farther north or south. This is because Earth is curved, and the sun's rays are more concentrated over the equator, where the sun is always high in the sky and directly overhead twice a year. Over **polar** areas, in the far north or south, the sun appears low in the sky in the summer months and does not appear at all in the winter.

Distance from the sea The oceans and seas have a modifying effect on the climate of places around them. The sea takes longer to heat up and cool down than the land. The air over the sea is usually similar to the temperature of the sea itself. Places close to the coast receive an "equable" climate as sea breezes keep them cooler in the summer and milder in the winter than places inland. Places inland have a more extreme climate with hotter summers and colder winters.

Different parts of Earth receive different amounts of light and energy from the sun—much of which is lost as it passes through the atmosphere.

The rays that reach Earth in northern or southern areas pass through a greater amount of atmosphere and lose more energy than the rays that reach Earth around the equator.

Around the northern and southern areas, rays are also dispersed over a larger area and heat the land less effectively than those near the equator.

Follow it through: inland and by the sea → Sea is more dense than the land → Sea heats and cools down more slowly than land

Altitude The sun heats land, and this, in turn, warms the air above it. The air at lower altitudes, where most of Earth's land can be found, is thicker and dustier than at higher altitudes and warms up more quickly. Because the air is thinner and cleaner higher up, it is not warmed as efficiently as the air below. Hills and mountains are therefore usually colder than land lower down.

Tanzania is near the equator and has a hot climate. On Mount Kilimanjaro, however, temperatures are much lower. At the very top, the land is covered in snow all year round.

Take it further
Glasgow in Scotland and Moscow in Russia are each about the same distance from the equator but have very different climates, because one is closer to the sea than the other. This affects the temperature and the amount of rainfall that they receive.

◆ Find these places in an atlas, do some research to find out the climate statistics for each city, and draw climate graphs—including temperature and rainfall for each month.
◆ What do you notice about the climate of each city?

In the summer, air over the sea is cooler than air over the land
In the winter, air over the sea is warmer than air over the land

Places close to the coast have an equable climate
Places inland have an extreme climate

Different vegetation occurs

PAST AND PRESENT CLIMATES

Earth's climate is constantly changing. Throughout history, there have been long periods when the climate has been cold and periods when it has been warm. These changes have a major impact on Earth's landscape.

Ice ages About every 100,000 years, over the last million years, Earth's average temperature has fallen by about 10 °F (5 °C), causing an ice age. Some of these ice ages lasted for thousands of years. The most recent, 20,000 years ago, is called the "Laurentide." Vast areas of Arctic seawater froze, and large areas of land experienced prolonged sub-zero temperatures and higher snowfalls.

A U-shaped valley in Norway, shaped thousands of years ago by the movement of an ice-age glacier.

Glaciers were formed by the snow, and these moved under pressure of the ice above it. Mountain glaciers moved down highland slopes, removing soil and wearing away rocks. The ice at the North Pole increased in size, its mass reaching 1,200 miles (2,000 km) farther south than it is today.

In northern **latitudes**, the effect of the ice ages on the landscape was considerable. Huge glaciers scoured the hills and valleys, removing soil and rock and dumping it several miles away, producing a variety of new features in the landscape.

Little ice ages Small drops in temperature of two or three degrees caused shorter periods of cold weather, such as the Little Ice Age of A.D. 1500 to 1700. Mountain glaciers advanced and rivers regularly froze so that "Frost Fairs"—markets and carnivals—became a feature of winter life on the river Thames in London, UK.

It is likely that ice ages will occur in the future as Earth's climate changes. Currently, Earth is experiencing a relatively warm period.

Follow it through: occurrence of ice ages

A change occurs in Earth's tilt, or sunspot activity changes

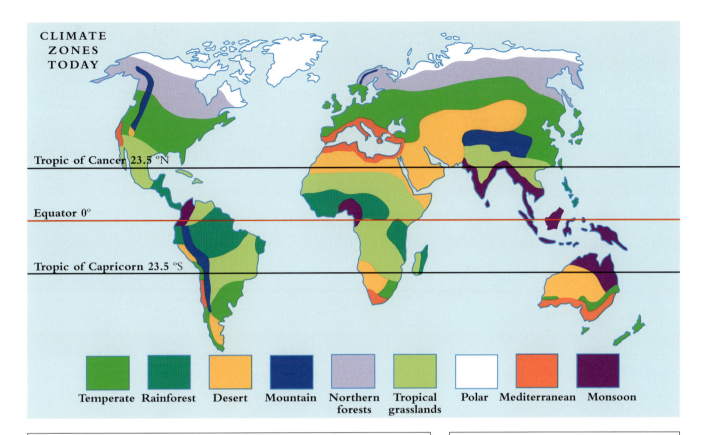

CLIMATE ZONES TODAY

Tropic of Cancer 23.5 °N
Equator 0°
Tropic of Capricorn 23.5 °S

Temperate | Rainforest | Desert | Mountain | Northern forests | Tropical grasslands | Polar | Mediterranean | Monsoon

Climate zones today There are nine "climate zones" on Earth—broad areas that have a similar climate (*see map above*). These areas also have similar vegetation and landscapes and are each explored further on pages 24–41.

Future climates?
Over the last 30 years, scientists have reported that Earth is getting warmer because of the increase in "greenhouse gases," such as carbon dioxide (*see pages 42–43*). They predict that the global temperature could rise by 5 °F (3 °C) by the end of the century, which could lead to the polar **ice caps** melting, rising sea levels submerging low land, a shifting of the world's climate patterns, and more extreme weather events. In the near future, Earth's climate zones map may look very different.

Case study: climate in the past
Earth's landscape itself can provide a lot of information about the climate in the past.

Geological: Glacier moraines (*see page 11*) often contain pollen, which gives information about the climate before and during the last ice age.
Ice: The analysis of the air trapped within ice can show the type and amount of different gases in the air at any time.
Tree rings: These can be used to see the weather over hundreds of years. Large gaps between the rings indicate wetter weather, and smaller gaps indicate drier weather.

Less heat comes from the sun → Earth's temperature falls → Ice age occurs

POLAR REGIONS

The polar regions in the Arctic and the Antarctic are the most northerly and southerly parts of Earth and experience the harshest climates in the world. They have an average temperature of less than 18 °F (10 °C) year-round. Ice polished by strong winds forms most of the landscape, making the poles inhospitable to vegetation, animals, and human life.

Emperor penguins in the Antarctic huddle together during a fierce storm.

Freezing cold At the poles, the sun is never high in the sky. The temperature remains below freezing for most of the year, especially when the sun dips below the horizon and the sky grows dark for six months (from March in Antarctica and from September in the Arctic).

The Antarctic The Antarctic is more inhospitable than the Arctic because it is a landmass and is an average of 8,200 feet (2,500 m) above sea level. It is almost completely covered by a thick layer of ice and snow, some of which is more than 15,400 feet (4,700 m) deep. It is the windiest place in the world. Occasionally, winds become hurricanes, which create vast areas of polished ice, worn smooth by ice crystals carried in the wind. The coldest temperature ever recorded was at Vostok in the Antarctic at -126 °F (-88 °C).

Follow it through: polar regions → Extremely cold climate → Permanent ice forms

Ice and rain Where the ice meets the sea, large chunks sometimes break off and float away as **icebergs**, leaving behind enormous ice cliffs. Only about five percent of the Antarctic is free of ice. Most of this is on the thin peninsula of land that reaches out toward South America. Underneath some of the ice lie lakes of fresh water.

Rainfall is rare and occurs only on the northern part of the Antarctica peninsula. There, some vegetation grows, including grass, moss, and lichen. Most precipitation is snow—about two inches (5 cm) a year inland and about 10 inches (25 cm) on the coast.

Take it further

Using resource material such as the Internet or reference books, trace an expedition to either the North or South Pole, perhaps by Shackleton, Scott, or Amundsen.

◆ Look at the route they took, the landscape they crossed, and the hardships they endured in order to reach the Pole.
◆ Look at how modern technology has made polar exploration easier than it was for explorers long ago.

An Antarctic iceberg breaking off from the Ross Ice Shelf.

The Arctic The Arctic, at the North Pole, is slightly warmer than the Antarctic, but still bitterly cold. It lies in a sea of permanent ice, touching land only in Greenland and the islands of northern Canada. The thinner ice over the ground around the edge of the Arctic melts during the short summer, but a few inches below the ground remains permanently frozen. This "permafrost" does not allow meltwater to soak away, so only a few plants, moss, lichens, and some grasses can grow.

The human landscape Life at the poles is difficult for people. In the Antarctic, there are no permanent settlements because of the climate and the lack of minerals and fossil fuels in the region. There are only temporary communities of scientists, working in isolated research stations.

The Arctic does have its own native people, the "Inuit," who were traditionally hunters, eating animal meat and using fur for clothing. In recent times, many have left their homelands to live in the towns of northern Canada. Of those that remain, only a few still hunt animals for their furs.

| The ground is permanently frozen | Meltwater cannot escape | Little vegetation can grow |

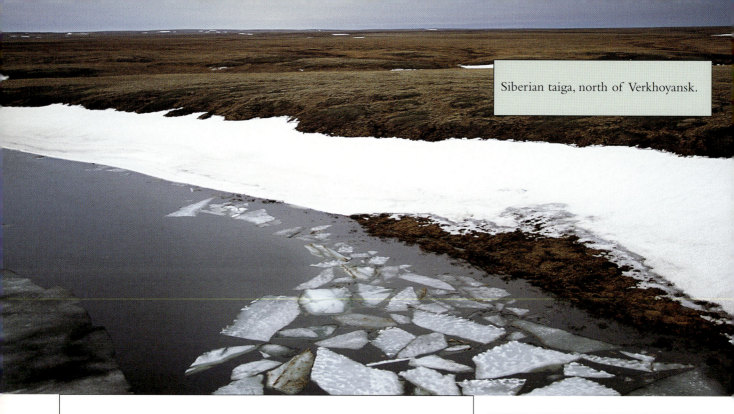

Siberian taiga, north of Verkhoyansk.

TAIGA (NORTHERN FORESTS)

The forests of the taiga stretch in a near continuous belt of coniferous trees across northern parts of America, Scandinavia, and Siberian Russia, and border the Arctic regions. (There are no true areas of taiga in the southern hemisphere.) These areas have long, severe winters, often with six months below freezing, and short summers. During the late spring and summer, the landscape is transformed—grasses, wild plants, and shrubs add to the greenery of the forests.

Temperature extremes The lowest recorded temperature (-90 °F/ -68 °C) outside of the Arctic was recorded at Verkhoyansk in the Siberian taiga. The clear winter skies and cold winds from the Arctic cause temperatures to fall to very low levels. The tree-covered landscape is covered with ice and snow from late autumn to early spring.

Because places far away from the sea experience a wide range of temperatures, Verkhoyansk can get quite hot in the summer months. The hottest recorded temperature there was 97 °F (36 °C).

Follow it through: northern forests → Long cold winters → Short growing season

Trees This heavily glaciated landscape of hills and valleys is largely covered by extensive forests of larch, pine, and spruce, with bogs occurring in poorly drained hollows left by glaciers. The trees are suited for survival in these inhospitable lands of extremes. They are conical in shape so they shed snow quickly, preventing the loss of branches, and they have needle leaves, often with waxy coatings, to prevent water loss and provide protection from the harsh, dry winds. They are evergreen so they can begin to make food as soon as it is warm enough in spring, and dark in color to help them absorb as much heat as possible.

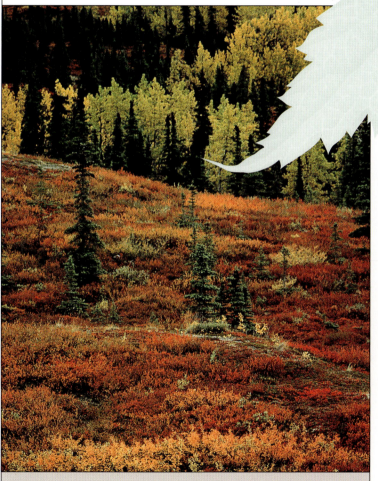

Autumn in Denali National Park, Alaska.

Take it further

In Alaska and Siberia, oil and gas fields have been developed to help supply the U.S. and Russia. Pipelines run above ground in the north of Alaska and to Valdez in the south. Service roads have been built next to them to provide easy access, if they should need to be repaired. An underground gas pipeline links Urengoi in central Russia with Germany toward the southwest.

◆ Use an atlas to determine how long each pipeline is and, looking at the landscape, suggest a route that each might follow.

Human life Life in the sparsely populated taiga is difficult. At -13 °F (-25 °C), diesel oil freezes, and at about -31 °F (-35 °C) human skin sticks to metal. People's homes in the established mining and fur trading centers are built with the harsh winter climate in mind. Houses have timber frames and are raised off the ground to prevent the warmth of the house from melting the permafrost and subsiding, and also so that the doorways can be cleared of snow. Houses usually have several layers of glass in their windows to help keep out the cold.

Coniferous trees suited to environment → Conical in shape to shed snow / Needle leaves to reduce loss of water / Evergreen so they make food as soon as possible → Northern forests

MOUNTAINS

Mountains are distributed around the world. Most mountains occur in chains or ranges that can run for hundreds or even thousands of miles. Their climate depends on altitude and aspect—the direction the sun is in. The climate of mountains is unique because it changes dramatically within a fairly short distance. Higher mountains have permanent snow on their summits, while their lower slopes will share the same climate as the land the mountain is situated in.

At the top It is always cold on the top of mountains, because the temperature falls by about 1.8 °F (1 °C) for every 330 feet (100 m) ascended. For that reason, the climate will be very different from that experienced lower down.

Toward the summit of the highest mountains, a layer of snow can be found that may have accumulated over hundreds of years. This will slowly change to ice and form a glacier that will eventually move downhill, forced by gravity and the weight of snow and ice above it.

As the glacier moves, it wears away the valley floors below, creating a variety of landscape features such as U-shaped valleys (*see page 11*) and hanging valleys with waterfalls. Hanging valleys are formed when the main valley and the valleys that enter it (tributary valleys) are eroded at different rates. The floors of the tributary valleys are deepened at a slower rate, so the difference between the depths of the two valleys increases over time. The tributaries are left high above the main valley, with their streams falling, sometimes almost vertically, into the larger valley below.

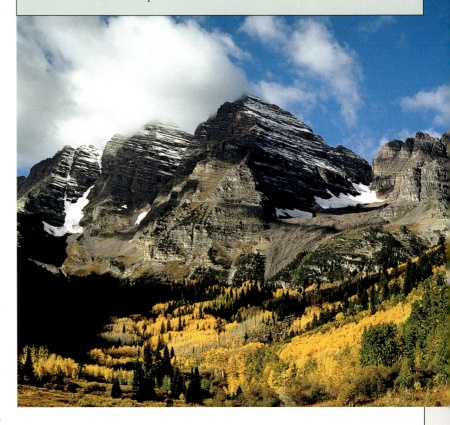

Autumn foliage at the bottom of this mountain in Colorado contrasts with the snow at the top.

Lower slopes On the lower slopes, broad-leaved trees can sometimes grow, while higher up, conifers survive until the climate becomes too cold for them. At this point, slow-growing alpine plants and grasses will be found. Higher still, where the climate is harsh, nothing will grow because the mountain slopes are composed of bare rock.

Case study: Chamonix, France

Chamonix is a French ski resort located about 50 miles (80 km) southeast of the city of Geneva in Switzerland. It is at the foot of Mont Blanc, which is the highest mountain in the Alps at 15,780 feet (4,810 m).

Tourist attraction

Chamonix attracts visitors at all times of the year. In the summer, people enjoy activities such as mountain biking and hiking. It is also a very popular winter ski resort. It has some of the longest ski runs in the Alps (105 miles/ 170 km), including some on glaciers.

Mountain changes

The town grew, like many others in the area, from a small village to a large modern resort. But tourism in this environment is a mixed blessing. On the one hand, tourists bring jobs to people who traditionally relied on sheep farming on the poor mountain soils. But delicate, slow-growing mountain plants were being destroyed by walkers and skiers. Walkers also exposed soil on footpaths, which were eroded with heavy rain. Soon Chamonix and other resorts in this area became the target for environmental protection groups. As a result, virtually no new ski resorts have been built in this part of the Alps for more than 20 years. Instead, efforts now go into improving those already there.

Take it further

Look at the summer and winter vacation brochures for a resort in the Alps.

- Choose a destination and hotel.
- Describe the landscape it is in and find out about the weather it receives in the winter and in the summer.

Skiers walk up "Vallée Blanche" in Chamonix, France. Constant use changes the landscape of the mountains.

TEMPERATE REGIONS

Temperate climates are those that do not have extremes of temperature or rainfall during the year and include most of Europe, New Zealand, East Asia, parts of Chile, and the northern U.S.

Inland or coastal There are differences in the climates of temperate regions. Those close to the sea have a "maritime" climate, where there is little difference in the winter and summer temperatures. Those farther inland have a "continental" climate, with warmer summers and colder winters. Places on the same latitude can therefore have noticeably different climates (*see pages 20–21*).

The Gulf Stream, a warm ocean current flowing north and east across the Atlantic Ocean from the Gulf of Mexico, helps to keep places in western Europe cooler in the summer and warmer in the winter than places inland and away from its influence. For example, Montreal in Canada has an average January temperature of 21 °F (-6 °C) and an average July temperature of 79 °F (26 °C), a range of 58 degrees. In Bordeaux, in western France, temperatures of 42 °F (6° C) and 70 °F (21 °C) are usual for the same months, a range of 28 degrees. Both of these places lie on the same latitude.

Farming Temperate regions experience the types of weather needed for successful farming, including mild to warm temperatures, rainfall all year-round, and many hours of sunshine. This has

Follow it through: temperate regions → Gentle climate → Good soil and weather for farming meant that the landscape in temperate areas has been dramatically altered by people, more so than many other areas.

Most of the natural vegetation of the temperate zones, such as broad-leaved trees (oak, elm, and ash), have been cleared for farming. In some parts of Canada and the U.S., for example, this has completely altered the landscape.

People places Although temperate regions cover only about eight percent of Earth's surface, they are home to about 40 percent of the world's population. This is due to the equable climate: neither too hot in the summer months, nor too cold during the winter, which makes living in the regions easier and more comfortable.

An increasing proportion of people living in temperate regions live in urban areas. This puts pressure on resources and the surrounding natural landscape. More land is needed for housing, industry, and transportation and to provide landfill sites. New sources of water have to be found or supplies brought in from other areas. These need to be stored, cleaned, and purified in reservoirs and treatment centers.

Much of the land in temperate regions is used for farming.

The population increases → Increased need for houses, work, and transportation → Pressure on the land

MEDITERRANEAN CLIMATE

The Mediterranean climate can be found in parts of the world between 30 and 50 degrees north and south of the equator, such as central and southern California, central Chile, southern Australia, the Cape area of South Africa, and lands that border the Mediterranean Sea. Mediterranean climates experience long, hot summers and mild winters.

Warm and dry In Mediterranean climates, temperatures rarely drop below 40 °F (5 °C) in the winter, while the average summer temperature reaches 80 °F (27 °C). Rainfall is fairly low, ranging between 11 and 24 inches (28–60 cm) a year. Frosts are rare, but when they do occur, they can cause great damage to the delicate crops that grow there.

The natural landscape of the Mediterranean regions is one of thick-barked coniferous trees, stunted evergreen oak, and sparse shrubs and grasses.

Farming Land around the Mediterranean is generally intensively cultivated because good farming land is fairly scarce. In many places, soils are poor and the land is rocky, so small areas of better land are not wasted. Even areas the size of a small garden may be planted with vegetable or salad crops.

Terraced fields, cut like steps into the sides of hills, are a common sight, since they conserve water from the limited rainfall. In the more fertile and larger fields in the valley floors, olives, grapes, citrus fruits, and wheat are grown. Because of the summer drought and high temperatures, most of these crops are irrigated to enable them to survive and ripen.

The natural landscape of these areas has, in many places, been altered by farmers, who have removed scrub and grasses for their crops.

A grove of irrigated orange trees in the Algarve, Portugal.

Wind damage Strong winds can sometimes cause considerable damage to crops, especially vines. Some Mediterranean countries suffer from the "Sirocco" (*see page* 7), a hot, dry wind that blows dust across the sea from the Sahara Desert in the south.

The "mistral" blows cold air north to south along the Rhone Valley in France, which acts as a wind tunnel for the strong, often hurricane-force, gusts. Again, this can cause great damage to newly planted crops.

The "Santa Ana" wind blows hot, dry air from the deserts of California, and other nearby states, causing damage to crops and bringing dust into the cities of the western coast. It also fans the flames of forest fires and can lead to the devastation of thousands of acres of natural woodland.

Vacation destination
The lands bordering the Mediterranean Sea have been an attractive destination to many people in Europe seeking a cheap vacation in almost guaranteed summer sunshine ever since affordable vacation packages became available in the 1970s. But, this has had a dramatic effect on these countries, particularly places on the coasts. Thousands of hotels and tourist attractions have sprung up, causing many changes to the areas.

Benidorm on the Costa Blanca of Spain has been changed dramatically by the influx of tourists attracted to its Mediterranean climate.

TROPICAL GRASSLANDS (SAVANNA)

The tropical grasslands, or savannas, are located between 10 and 20 degrees north and south of the equator and include parts of India and West Africa, northern Australia, and parts of South America, such as the "cerrado" of Brazil. Rain falls for most of the year, but there is a dry season. Temperatures average between 77 and 86 °F (25 to 30 °C) all year-round. The landscape consists of a vast area of grassland punctuated with occasional drought-resistant trees and shrubs.

Wet and dry seasons The climate of the savanna has distinct wet and dry seasons, with most rainfall occurring in the summer months.

During the dry season, temperatures may be around 68 to 72 °F (20 to 22 °C), rising to 77 to 86 °F (25 to 30 °C) just before the rains arrive. At this time, the grass is brown and dry and almost completely lacking in nutrients, while the soil is baked hard. Most rain falls in the form of thunderstorms, with torrential rain over the course of just a few weeks. Up to 39 inches (1 m) of rain can fall in this time.

Much of this rainfall collects in hollows to form shallow lakes and pools, because the rain cannot easily soak through the hard baked ground. The rain transforms the landscape: dry grasses and plants quickly put on lush new growth, and dormant seeds burst into life.

A storm gathers over the savanna in the Masai Mara, Kenya.

Follow it through: Serengeti changes → South of region is lush and green, animals graze → Rains move north

Case study: the Serengeti National Park, Tanzania

The Serengeti National Park is one of the most famous wildlife sanctuaries in the world. *Serengeti* is a Masai word meaning "endless plains"—appropriate since this part of the savanna covers an area of 5,700 square miles (14,763 sq km). It is home to more than three million large mammals that roam the plains in total freedom.

The grasslands are broken up by "kopjes" (pronounced copies)—rounded granite rock outcrops which are the result of cracking and erosion from exposure to the sun, wind, and rain. There are patches of acacia, broad-topped drought-resistant woodland, and swamps and lakes that fill and empty with the passing of the seasons.

The Serengeti changes with the passing rain. In May in southern Tanzania, the grasses start to disappear, and the giant herds move north, following the storm clouds to fresh grazing. By November, these grasses are exhausted, and the herds return to the south where the whole cycle begins again.

A kopje, or small hill, in the Serengeti National Park, Tanzania.

Game reserves Game reserves, including the Serengeti in Tanzania, the Masai Mara in Kenya, and those in Botswana, Zimbabwe, and South Africa, are most closely associated with the landscape of the savanna. Throughout these areas, there is a continuous cover of grasses, often more than three feet (1 m) tall. Trees are sparse in this semi-arid landscape, growing only where there are cracks in the brick-hard ground or where there is deep soil. The acacia tree is found in East Africa, as well as thorn bushes, palms, and some fruit trees, which provide food and shade for a wide variety of animals and birds.

In the south, vegetation dies out
North becomes lush → Animals move north → The grasses in the north are exhausted → Animals move south to new pastures, following the rain again

DESERTS

Desert landscapes are found throughout the world. They occur in areas where the rainfall is less than 10 inches (25 cm) a year. In hot deserts, where evaporation is high, hardly any vegetation is able to survive. In some deserts, years can pass with no rainfall at all. In fact, parts of the Atacama Desert in Chile are said to have had no rainfall for more than a hundred years.

Hot deserts Hot deserts occur mainly between 15 and 30 degrees north and south of the equator. Deserts cover about 14 percent of Earth's surface. The Sahara is the largest desert in the world with an area slightly greater than the U.S.

Hot deserts experience extremely high temperatures during the day, often close to 122 °F (50 °C), and low temperatures during the night, because there are usually no clouds to stop the daytime heat from escaping.

Cold deserts Not all deserts are hot—the Gobi Desert is a cold desert. It lacks rain because the winds that cross the desert are dry; any rain that they carry falls near coastal areas. Winters are cold, and although summers are warm, they are short, and little rain falls.

Monument valley, Navajo Tribal Park, Utah.

Striking formations Because of the harsh climate, desert landscapes are unique and striking. With virtually no vegetation, the actual colors of the land can be seen. Rocky deserts may be punctuated with "inselbergs," or "island mountains," of harder, more resistant rock, and flat-topped hills called "mesas" and "buttes," which are found in North American deserts.

Follow it through: desertification → Farmers need land for grazing animals → Trees are removed

Some parts of the Sahara are crisscrossed with "wadis"—dry, steep-sided river valleys that can quickly fill with water after a storm, and then just as quickly empty and dry up.

In sandy deserts, features are produced by the wind blowing sand into crescent-shaped dunes called "barchans" or long, thin "seif dunes" which move slowly in the direction of the prevailing wind.

Dust storms are common in deserts. They occur quickly and are hot and abrasive, preventing people from traveling or even going outside.

After spring rains, Californian poppies burst into life in the Mojave Desert, California.

Plants Plants in the desert tend to be ground-hugging shrubs and stumpy trees with small, thick leaves to help conserve water. The seeds of some plants lie on the ground, often for years, waiting for the rain to come. When it does, they grow and flower quickly, transforming the hostile landscape into a carpet of color.

Desertification People have played a major part in increasing the size of many deserts by removing trees and allowing their animals to overgraze the sparse vegetation. Trees not only help to bind the poor soils together but also increase the amount of water vapor in the air.

Creating desert from semi-arid regions bordering deserts is called desertification. It is currently happening in the Sahel region, which borders the Sahara Desert in Africa. When an area changes to desert, it is difficult to return it to its previous state, although irrigation and **afforestation**, tree-planting programs, have had some success.

Tree roots no longer hold the soil together → The soil erodes → Land turns to desert → Farmers move to a new area

RAINFORESTS

Tropical rainforest in St. Lucia, West Indies.

The rainforest stretches in a broad belt around the middle of Earth within 10 and 15 degrees north and south of the equator. It includes the giant river basins of the Amazon in South America, the Congo in Central Africa, Central America, Southeast Asia, and northern Australia.

Rain and sun Rain occurs on most days, usually in the form of heavy thunderstorms that rattle around the forest, soaking the trees and the ground. Each day begins sunny and hot, the damp ground from the previous day's rain slowly evaporates, and cumulus clouds begin to develop. These darken, and by the late afternoon or early evening, rain begins to fall—leaving the nights clear and dry.

An orangutan in a rainforest in Borneo.

Follow it through: rainforest climate → Trees cleared for farming → Plant roots no longer draw up water

Plants As a result, plants and trees cover the landscape. There is no winter, and the temperature in the rainforest is more or less the same every day, varying by only about 4 °F (2 °C) over the year from an average of about 82 °F (28 °C). Plants can therefore grow, flower, and fruit at any time so that the rainforest is always lush and green.

Local climate For many years, rainforests have been cleared for farming and mining. In the long-term, this may have an effect on the climate of the tropics. Plant roots draw up water from the ground. Water evaporates from the surface of their leaves, turning to vapor and mixing with the air. This helps to form the clouds, and the rain falls back on the forest again. With fewer trees, less water evaporates, so less falls as rain. The climate of the rainforest may change so that instead of daily rainfall, there may be droughts.

Wind and rain damage When trees are removed, the soil may be eroded by wind and heavy rain. This leaves only small patches of rainforest, which may not survive.

Global climate As well as altering the local climate, the destruction of the rainforests may also affect the global climate, because less carbon dioxide is absorbed from the atmosphere and less oxygen is returned to it (*see page 42*).

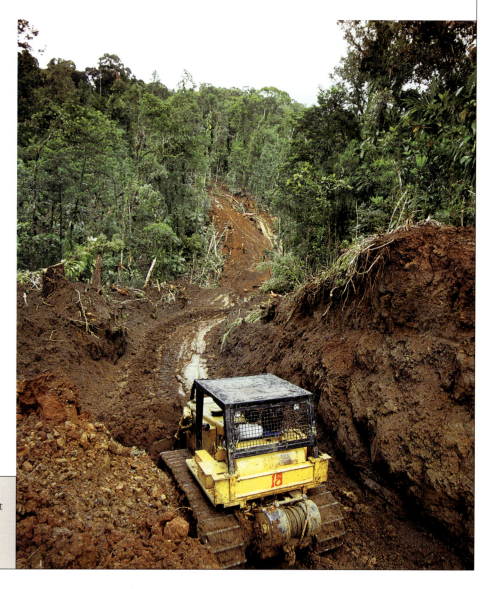

The destruction of the rainforest for farming, mining, and roads threatens rainforest climates.

| Less water evaporates into the atmosphere from leaves | Fewer clouds are formed | Less rain, so the vegetation changes further |

MONSOON LANDS

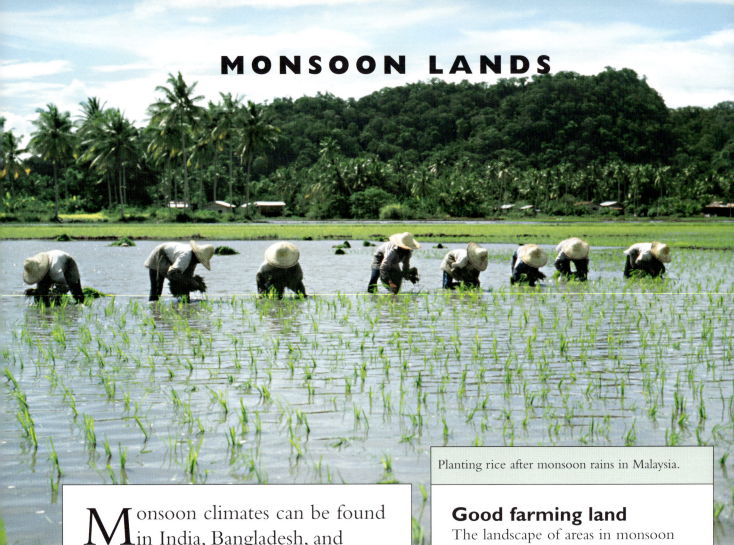

Planting rice after monsoon rains in Malaysia.

Monsoon climates can be found in India, Bangladesh, and Southwest Asia, and in the tropical regions of West Africa, northern Australia, and western Columbia. The term "monsoon" was used by Arab sailors to describe the shifting winds that blow over the Indian Ocean and the Arabian Sea. In parts of India, the monsoon can be very dramatic—some places may receive three-quarters of their annual rainfall in just three months.

Good farming land

The landscape of areas in monsoon climates is one of tropical evergreen trees interspersed with occasional grasslands, much of which is farmed. Large amounts of rice are cultivated in these regions, and farmers rely on the cycle of the monsoon and the rains that it brings to produce a good crop of rice.

The monsoon rain can also be destructive for farming, however. The soil can easily be washed away by the heavy rain, so farmers have to take measures to protect it, such as terracing and building earth banks to prevent run-off.

Follow it through: monsoon → Stable air covers the Indian sub-continent → The sun heats the land, temperatures rise

Case study: the Indian monsoon

In March and April, the heat in India begins to build so that by May some of the highest temperatures of the year occur. As the land heats up, there is an ever-increasing difference between the temperature of the land and the temperature of the sea. The mass of hot air over the land rises, and cooler moist air from over the sea is drawn in to take its place. The land warms this air, and it rises quickly and then cools and condenses, causing droplets of water to merge and form raindrops which eventually fall to the ground as torrential rain.

Himalaya region

The south and west of India receive most of the country's monsoon rainfall. There, the monsoon is more dramatic than anywhere else in the world. The mountains of the Himalayas and the Hindu Kush trap the moisture over the sub-continent, allowing the monsoon to continue for several months.

Disasters

With a population of about one billion people, a failure of the monsoon can ruin harvests and cause widespread famine as crops wither in parched fields. Too much rain, however, may bring catastrophic flooding, causing thousands of people to lose their lives as huge expanses of fertile, productive land are covered in an enormous floodwater lake.

A dark, stormy sky at the arrival of the Indian monsoon.

Strong winds blow inshore from the southwest → Storm clouds develop → Monsoon occurs

THE FUTURE

Changes in the heat produced by the sun cause the climate to change naturally, but over the last 30 years, many scientists have reported that Earth is getting warmer due to the increase in "greenhouse gases." They are concerned that this will cause changes to the world's weather and even eventually change our climate.

What is global warming?

Greenhouse gases are carbon dioxide, nitrous oxide, and methane. These are produced by human activity—burning fossil fuels such as coal, the fumes from car exhausts, and the spread of intensive agriculture. The gases combine to reduce the amount of heat escaping from Earth's surface and cause it to become warmer.

Another problem is deforestation. Trees absorb carbon dioxide and release oxygen. Deforestation across vast areas of the world, especially in the rainforests, has reduced Earth's ability to remove the excess carbon dioxide in the atmosphere.

Pollution from industry is thought to be one of the causes of global warming.

Follow it through: global warming → Destruction of forests / Increased use of fossil fuel / Increased use of cars → Increase in greenhouse gases

What is the effect? Although virtually all scientists agree that Earth is getting warmer, they disagree on how much the temperature will rise and what the effects of this might be. The most reliable predictions say that a 5.5 °F (3 °C) rise is likely before the end of this century.

As the temperature of Earth rises, scientists suggest that the ice caps over the North and South Poles will melt, sea levels will rise, and there will be an increase in extreme weather events. Low-lying coastal areas will come under threat from the sea, especially during storm surges, and some islands will disappear. The amount of rainfall Earth receives is expected to increase overall, especially in Central Africa and high northern latitudes. However, in some places, such as southern Europe, southern Africa, Australia, and Central America, rainfall will decrease.

Global warming may, over time, alter the size and distribution of many of Earth's climatic zones. For example, there may be new areas of desert, existing desert areas may receive more rainfall, and temperate regions may become more Mediterranean in character, with higher summer and winter temperatures.

What is being done? In 1997, at the Kyoto Climate Summit, more than 1,500 scientists called on the world's governments to take action to reduce levels of human-induced global warming and to show a new commitment to protecting the global environment.

Despite scientists' concerns, governments of some countries are reluctant to enforce a reduction of greenhouse gas emissions because they fear that it will make products more expensive, put people out of work, and harm their economies.

Take it further

Find out what you can about greenhouse gases, how they are caused, and the effect they have on Earth's climate.

◆ Make an information leaflet outlining the facts, your concerns, and suggestions as to how to create a better future for everyone.

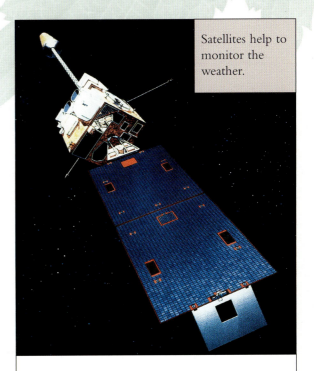

Satellites help to monitor the weather.

Forecasting Inventions such as weather satellites will help keep track of any changes to global weather patterns. They monitor snow and ice cover, as well as sea surface temperature, and provide information on what is happening to the world. We have the technology and the ability to slowly change our climate; the question is, how much do we really want to?

Increase in temperature → Melting ice caps, rises in sea levels → More extreme weather events

GLOSSARY

Acid rain	Rain that contains sulphuric and nitric acid that may damage vegetation and life in streams and lakes over time.
Afforestation	Large-scale tree-planting.
Air pressure	The weight of the atmosphere pressing on Earth's surface.
Atmosphere	A blanket of air about 60 miles (100 km) thick that encircles Earth.
Clouds	Dense masses of water droplets and/or ice crystals visible in the sky.
Drought	A long, continuous period of dry weather.
Equator	An imaginary line running east and west around the center of Earth.
Glaciers	Slow-moving rivers of ice.
Gorges	Narrow, steep-sided river valleys.
Humid	Full of water vapor.
Hurricane	An intense, spinning storm with violent winds and torrential rain.
Ice age	A time in Earth's history when thick ice sheets covered much of the mid-latitudes (40–60 degrees) in the northern hemisphere.
Ice cap	A permanent covering of ice—such as at the poles.
Iceberg	A mass of ice that has broken away from an ice sheet.
Irrigation	Taking water to dry land through channels, sprinklers, and hoses.
Landscape	The characteristics that comprise any given area of land on Earth.
Latitudes	Imaginary circles drawn around Earth in an east–west direction.
Meanders	Winding curves in the course of a river.
Mountain	A mass of land more than 980 feet (300 m) high.
Polar	Relating to one of the two ends (the North Pole and the South Pole) of the imaginary axis on which Earth turns.
Rapids	Areas of fast-flowing river water.
Stalactites	Columns of pure limestone hanging from the roof of a cave.
Stalagmites	Columns of pure limestone formed on the floor of a cave.

Tornadoes Violently whirling, funnel-shaped clouds that usually destroy everything in their paths.

Waterfalls Points on a river where the water falls vertically.

FURTHER INFORMATION

National Weather Service
Official Web site for the U.S. National Weather Service, with information on forecasts, warnings, weather safety, and satellite images.

www.nws.noaa.gov

Friends of the Earth International
A coalition of worldwide environmental groups, working on many environmental issues, including climate change.

www.foei.org

Greenpeace International
A global organization that works to protect the planet's biodiversity and environment.

www.greenpeace.org

Weather extremes
The Web site of the National Oceanic and Atmospheric Administration can be used to find out about extreme weather conditions, and when they are likely to strike next.

www.noaa.gov/wx.html

Weather satellite images
The Web site of NASA's Global Hydrology and Climate Center has interactive satellite images.

www.ghcc.msfc.nasa.gov/ghcc_home.html

World climate
This site offers a weather information service for many towns and cities worldwide.

www.worldclimate.com

INDEX

Africa 14–18, 32, 34, 35, 37, 38, 40, 43
air pressure 6, 7, 16, 17, 19, 44
Alaska 27
altitude 21, 28
America 10, 26, 36
Antarctic 24, 25
Arctic 20, 22, 24, 25, 26
Asia 18, 30, 38, 40
atmosphere 6, 7, 8, 20, 39, 42, 44
Australia 16, 32, 34, 38, 40, 43

Canada 10, 17, 25, 30, 31
Central America 38, 43
climate 6, 20–25, 28, 30–34, 36, 38–40, 42–43
cloud 6, 7, 17, 19, 36, 38, 39, 41, 44
coast 10, 13, 17, 20, 21, 25, 30, 33, 36, 43
conifer 26–28, 32
corrie 10, 11

desert 7, 8, 11, 14, 15, 20, 23, 33, 36–37, 43
desertification 37
drought 14–15, 18, 19, 32, 34, 35, 39, 44
dune 11, 37

Egypt 15
El Niño 18–19
equator 14, 20, 21, 23, 32, 34, 36, 38, 44
erosion 6, 10–11, 14, 35, 39

famine 19
farming 14, 30–33, 36, 38–40
flood 12–13, 15, 17–19, 41
forest 19, 26, 27, 38, 39, 42
  fire 19, 33
France 29, 30, 33

game reserve 35
Germany 13, 27
glaciation 10, 27
glacier 10, 11, 22, 23, 27–29, 44

global warming 23, 39, 42–43
greenhouse gas 23, 42, 43
Gulf Stream 30

hurricane 6, 13, 16–17, 24, 33, 44

ice 10, 11, 22–26, 28, 43, 44
ice age 10, 22, 23, 44
ice cap 23, 43, 44
India 34, 40, 41
Indonesia 18, 19
irrigation 15, 32, 37, 44
Italy 8, 12

La Niña 18
landscape 6–8, 10, 12, 14, 15, 17, 20, 22–24, 26–28, 30–32, 34–37, 39, 40, 44
latitude 30, 43, 44
limestone 9, 45

Mediterranean 6, 7, 23, 32–33, 43
monsoon 23, 40–41
moraine 11, 23
Mount Kilimanjaro 21
mountain 8, 10, 11, 21–23, 28–29, 41, 44, 45
mudslide 12, 18, 19

northern forest. See taiga

Pacific Ocean 16, 18, 19
polar region 10, 20, 23, 24–25
poles, the 24, 25, 43, 44
Prague 13

rainfall 6, 7, 9, 11–15, 18, 19, 21, 25, 30, 32, 34, 36, 39–41, 43, 45
rainforest 20, 23, 38–39, 42
river 9, 11, 12, 15, 22, 35–38, 44, 45
rock 8–9, 10–12, 22, 28, 41
Russia 13, 21, 26, 27

Sahara Desert 6, 7, 33, 36, 37
sand 7, 9, 11, 37
Saudi Arabia 15
savanna 34–35

scree 8
sea 10, 12, 13, 15, 17, 18, 20–26, 30, 32, 36, 41, 43
season 6, 8, 34, 35
Siberia 26, 27
Sirocco 6, 7, 33, 34, 35
snow 10, 11, 21, 22, 24–28, 43
soil 10–14, 22, 29, 30, 32, 34, 35, 37, 39, 40
South America 18, 25, 30, 32, 34, 36, 38
Sri Lanka 15
storm 7, 13, 16, 17, 19, 24, 37, 41, 44
storm surge 17, 43
sun 6, 7, 8, 20, 21, 23, 24, 28, 30, 34, 35, 38, 40, 42

taiga 26–27
Tanzania 15, 21, 35
temperate region 23, 30–31, 43
temperature 6–8, 12, 14, 18, 19, 20, 21, 22, 23, 24, 26, 28, 30, 32, 34, 36, 39, 40, 41, 42, 43
thunderstorm 7, 34, 38
tornado 16–17, 19, 45
tree 7, 12–14, 17, 23, 26, 27, 31, 34–40, 42, 44
tropical grassland 23, 34–35

UK (United Kingdom) 9, 13, 22
U.S. (United States of America) 11, 17, 18, 19, 27, 30–33, 36, 37

valley 8, 10, 11, 22, 27, 28, 32, 33, 37, 44
vegetation 14, 21, 23–25, 31, 36, 37, 39, 44

water 9–12, 14, 15, 18, 19, 25, 27, 31, 37–39, 44
  shortage of 14–15
weather pattern 6, 20, 43
weathering 6, 7, 8–9, 10
wind 6, 7, 10, 11, 16, 17, 19, 24, 26, 27, 33, 35–37, 39, 40, 41, 44, 45

Yorkshire Dales 9